Adventure
Stories

Written by Jan Astley, Becky Brookes,
Gaby Goldsack, Kath Jewitt,
Paeony Lewis, Sue Nicholson,
Ronne Randall and Louisa Somerville

Illustrated by John MacGregor

Designed by Blue Sunflower Creative

This edition published by Parragon in 2010
Parragon
Queen Street House
4 Queen Street
Bath BA1 1HE, UK

ISBN 978-1-4054-7623-2

Printed in China

Adventure
Stories

PaRragon

Bath · New York · Singapore · Hong Kong · Cologne · Delhi · Melbourne

Contents

Sammy the Super-detective

Sammy dropped down on her knees and crawled along behind the hedge.

But it was too late. She'd been spotted. "Is that you, Sammy Dunton?" called her mum. "Come out from behind that hedge. I can see you, you know."

"Oops," muttered Sammy. It looked as though she was never going to find out where her birthday present was hidden. It was even harder that her house was also a guest house – *Sea View Guest House*, as there were so many rooms to check.

"You're just a nosy parker," laughed Mrs Dunton, as Sammy clambered to her feet.

"I'm not," Sammy declared. "I'm just

curious. And you need to be curious when you're a super-detective, like I am."

"Super-detective?" laughed Mrs Dunton. "Is that what you're calling yourself nowadays? You look more like a little girl in dirty jeans to me."

Sammy pulled herself upright and stuck her nose in the air. "Yes, I am a super-detective," she said grandly. "Look, I've even got a detective pad and a magnifying glass. They came in a special kit Dad gave me."

"Well, you have fun playing detectives. But please don't bother the guests. Mr Black in Room 10 has complained that you've been spying on him through your binoculars again."

Sammy marched off crossly. Nobody took her detective work seriously. Everyone just laughed and patted her on the head. They seemed to forget about all the mysteries she had solved. After all, she had been the one who had discovered it was the squirrels stealing her mum's carrots. And it had been she who had set a trap and caught Bruno the dog running off with the guests' post.

"I'm a great detective. And one of these days, everyone will realize that," Sammy muttered. She sat down on her swing and took out her notepad and pencil. She watched the guest house for a while and then began to take notes.

2pm - Dad takes out the rubbish.

2.02pm - Dad comes back from taking out rubbish.

2.05pm - Bruno sniffs tree, then goes to his kennel.

2.08pm - Mum comes out and starts to clean windows.

2.10pm - Mr Black leaves the hotel. Note to self - must watch that one. Wears dark glasses and has a moustache. Certainly up to no good.

2.15pm - Hear scream from hotel. Better go and see what's wrong...

Sammy rushed into the guest house, just as Mrs Pringle from Room 5 rushed up to the reception desk. The small, grey-haired old lady was shaking and clutching her heart.

"H…h…help! My diamond ring has vanished. It's worth a small fortune. I think your dog might have taken it. Remember the time he stole all the post? Call the police! Call the fire brigade! Call the ambulance! Call somebody!" she kept ranting at Sammy's Dad.

"Now take a deep breath and start at the beginning," said Mr Dunton kindly. "Did I hear you say something about a missing ring?"

"Yes, of course you did. My diamond

ring has gone. One moment it was on the side of the basin and the next it was gone. I think your dog took it. I just saw him leave my room and he looked pretty guilty to me. In fact, I would bet it was that mangy mutt that swallowed it!"

"Perhaps I can be of some assistance," interrupted Sammy, stepping up beside the old lady and taking her elbow. "It can't have been Bruno because…"

"Not now, dear," said Mrs Pringle. "This is grown-up stuff." The old lady turned back to Mr Dunton and continued. "I wouldn't make such a fuss," she said. "But it's the most valuable thing I have. It's worth thousands."

"Don't worry," said Mr Dunton. "We'll call the police and search this place high and low. We'll even follow Bruno to see if – ahem…" Mr Dunton coughed delicately and looked embarrassed, "…he's eaten it and, you know…we'll do whatever we have to do to get to the bottom of this situation."

Sammy started to giggle. Mr Dunton and Miss Pringle frowned at her crossly.

"Well," said Mrs Pringle, still glaring at Sammy. "I'm afraid that if it doesn't turn up, I'm going to have to ask you to pay for a new ring. I wouldn't like to do it but I'm just a poor old widow living on my pension."

"Of course, of course," said Mr Dunton, who was already dialling the police.

A few hours later, Sammy stood at the top of the stairs, eavesdropping on the conversation between a policeman and her dad. "No sign of forced entry," said the policeman. "No strange fingerprints. No mess. It looks like an inside job to me. And as we know from your daughter's notes that you and your wife were all outside, everything points to the dog. He does have a history of theft," he finished.

Sammy raced down the stairs and tugged at the policeman's sleeve. "But Bruno was in his kennel when it happened," she cried.

"Can you actually prove that?" asked the policeman. "Were you with him for the whole time."

"N...o," replied Sammy slowly. "But I saw him go into the kennel."

"Well, he could have snuck out again and run upstairs while you weren't looking, couldn't he? After all, you were busy watching everyone else."

"Yeah, I suppose he could have," replied Sammy. "But I'm sure he wouldn't have gone into Mrs Pringle's room. I don't think he likes her perfume and he avoids her as much as possible. What about Mr Black? He could have taken the ring. He was seen leaving the scene of the crime at about the right time."

The policeman began to fiddle with his uniform buttons and looked uncomfortable. "It wasn't Mr Black. I know that for a fact. Just take my word for it. As I said before, everything points to the dog!"

The next morning at breakfast, Mr and Mrs Dunton were very quiet. Sammy had followed Bruno like a shadow and was sure that he hadn't – ahem – left anything. The ring was still missing and it looked like Mr and Mrs Dunton were going to have to foot the bill for a new one.

After breakfast, Sammy went up to her room and found the special 'Super-detective' kit that her dad had bought her. She rifled through the box, until she found what she was looking for – an enormous hat, a surprisingly hairy moustache and a pair of ridiculously large sunglasses. She put them on and looked in the mirror.

"Perfect," she smiled. "Nobody will recognize me in this clever disguise." And, without further ado, she set off to clear Bruno's name!

Taking great care not to be seen, Sammy darted out of the house and hid behind the apple tree. She waited there until Mr Black left the guest house. As he walked out of the gate, Sammy counted to twenty, then began to follow him.

Sammy trailed Mr Black down the road and along the high street, dodging between lamp posts, letter boxes and anything else she could find to hide behind. Suddenly, Mr Black whirled around and stared in Sammy's direction. Thankful for her disguise, Sammy simply stared right back and carried on walking. When they were nearly face-to-face, Mr Black swung around and continued on his way.

"Phew," thought Sammy. "That was close. Thank goodness for my cunning disguise."

Sammy carried on following Mr Black, until he ducked into a building that she'd never seen before. Feeling safe in her disguise, Sammy walked to the front of the building and bent back her head to read the sign over its front door.

"P.O.L.I.C.E…" read Sammy out loud.

"Yes. Police Station," said a voice behind her.

Sammy gasped and twirled round. It was Mr Black. He'd known he was being followed all the time.

"Why are you following me, Sammy?" he asked. He took off his glasses and smiled at her kindly.

"Err. My name's not Sammy," lied Sammy. "I'm Mr…Mr…Brown."

"Oh, come off it, Sammy," laughed Mr Black. "Anyone can see it's you under that silly disguise. And it looks like you've discovered my little secret."

Suddenly, Sammy felt just a tiny bit afraid. What little secret was he talking about? Oh, dear! It looked as though she'd got herself into BIG trouble this time.

"Secret? Secret? I don't know anything about secrets. I don't know what you are talking about," she gabbled. She whisked

off her disguise and started
to walk backwards. "I'm
just a silly little girl. Why
would I care that you're
a nasty old, ring-
stealing crook?"

Mr Black
began to laugh
harder than
ever.

"Sammy,
I'm not a crook.
I'm a policeman.
A plain-clothes detective. That's the secret
I'm talking about."

For once, Sammy was lost for words.
Mr Black was a detective! But why, if he
was a detective, was he pretending to be a
guest at *Sea View Guest House*? Sammy
shook her head and looked confused.

Mr Black led her into the police

station, where he explained that he was working under cover.

"I have reason to believe that Mrs Pringle isn't who she says she is," he explained. "In fact, she isn't a sweet old lady at all. She's Diamond Di, a well-known diamond thief and all-round crook."

"But what's she doing in our guest house?" asked Sammy.

"I believe that she's trying to con money out of your parents. I don't think there ever was a diamond ring. I think she's pretending Bruno took one to get your parents to give her some cash!"

"Wow!" Sammy couldn't believe her ears. They had a real, live villain staying in their guest house. And, what was worse, she was trying to swindle Sammy's parents.

"I won't let her get away with this!" Sammy cried.

"Neither will I," said Mr Black. "And I

have a cunning plan. All we need to do is to wave a diamond ring under Diamond Di's nose and she won't be able to resist temptation. She will unmask herself by trying to steal it, I'm sure."

"Will this do?" asked Sammy, tugging something out of her pocket. It twinkled under the harsh overhead light. It was a glass spy ring that had come with her detective kit. 'Sparkles like a real diamond' it had said on the pack.

Mr Black, or as Sammy now knew him, 'Detective Black', picked up the ring and smiled.

"This looks like the very thing we need," he grinned.

Later that evening, while Mrs Pringle was sitting in the lounge, Sammy wandered in and dropped the ring on the sideboard. Then she left the room, and squeezed in beside Mr Black behind the door.

They didn't have to wait long. As soon as Mrs Pringle caught sight of the sparkly ring, her eyes lit up. In a flash, she leapt to her feet, grabbed the ring and stuffed it in her pocket.

"You move pretty fast for a pensioner," announced Mr Black, stepping out from behind the door. "But not fast enough."

He grabbed Mrs Pringle and had her handcuffed in a few seconds. "Diamond Di, you are under arrest for theft and deception."

"I think you've got something of mine," added Sammy, in her deepest, most important super-detective voice, stepping forward to take back her pretend diamond ring from the thief.

"Oh, you," said Diamond Di looking at Sammy as if she was something horrid. "But how did you know it was me?" she asked, in a voice that didn't sound at all like the old

Mrs Pringle. She shook her head crossly and her curly grey wig flew off. Beneath it she had short, spiky hair. She had been in disguise all along!

"I've been watching you for months," said Mr Black. "But I'd never have caught you if it hadn't been for my pal here, Detective Sammy Dunton."

Sammy blushed with pleasure.

She really was a Super-detective.

Now, if she could just find out where her birthday present was hidden…

Robert and the Magic Helmet

Robert stood as straight and tall as he could, while his mum measured him against the height chart.

"114 centimetres!" said his mum. "You've grown four centimetres in the last two months. You should be really pleased."

But Robert wasn't pleased.

"What's wrong?" asked Mum.

"I'm a titch!" said Robert. "No matter how much I grow, I'm still shorter than Tom and Danny. I'll never be as tall as my friends. I feel like a loser!"

"You're not a loser at all," said Mum. "You don't have to be tall to be a winner. Anyone can be a big person on the inside, and remember," she finished, smiling, "if your legs are long enough to reach the ground, you're just fine!"

"Mu-um," groaned Robert, "you always say that – and it doesn't help!" He stomped out of his room, clomped downstairs, and flopped down in front of the TV. There was a football match on, and he didn't want to miss it.

Robert loved football almost as much as he hated being short. But when his friends got together to play, Robert never joined them. They were all so much bigger and taller than he was – he was worried that he couldn't run as fast as they could, or that he wasn't as strong as they were. And what if someone tackled him? He would get trampled! So he always made up an excuse when they asked him to play.

But he loved watching football and keeping up with his favourite team, Castleton United. His room was decorated in blue and gold, Castleton's colours, and he and his dad went to nearly every home match. When Castleton played an away match, as they were doing today, Robert watched the match on TV.

For almost two hours, Robert sat glued to the television set, watching the Castleton players storm down the pitch. He dreamed of being just like them – but when he remembered how small he was, his heart sank.

The next day was Sunday, and after lunch, Robert decided to ride his bike down to the park. As he got there, he saw some boys he knew from school, along with his friends Tom and Danny.

"Hey, Robert!" called Danny. "We're getting teams together for a five-a-side match. Come on – we need you to play!"

Part of Robert desperately wanted to join them. But another part was scared.

What if he couldn't run as fast as the bigger boys? What if his short legs tripped over the ball? What if the big boys on the other team laughed at him? What if he lost the match for his team and his friends got angry with him?

"Uhhhh...sorry," said Robert. "I have to run an errand for my mum. Can't play. See ya!" And he zoomed off on his bike before they could say another word.

Trying not to cry, Robert rode out of the park. He wasn't sure where to go next. If he went home, his parents would wonder why he was back so soon. And it was Sunday, so the newsagent would have closed at lunchtime – he couldn't even buy a football magazine with his pocket money.

Robert rode to the shops anyway, and was surprised to see that one was open. It was a dusty old junk shop he'd never paid any attention to before. But now, with nothing else to do, he stopped to look at the collection of odd objects that were set out in front.

There was a chest with flowers painted on the front, and sitting on top of it was a ship in a big bottle. There was a broken old rocking chair, and there were a couple of crates of old books. Robert began looking through them to see if there were any about football. There weren't, but he did find an interesting old book with a faded tan cover called *Knights of Old*. Robert picked it up and began leafing through it.

Soon he was lost in the pictures of stone castles and knights in armour. His attention was caught by a picture of a knight on a white horse sinking his spear into a fire-breathing dragon.

"If only I were that big," sighed Robert to himself. "Then maybe I would be that brave, too."

When he looked up from the book, Robert noticed something shiny in the window of the shop. To his amazement, it was a metal helmet, just like the one the knight in the book was wearing!

Eager to have a closer look, Robert went into the shop. It was dark and dusty, and at first it seemed that no one was there. But then a grey-haired woman emerged from the back. She wore a dark green dress and a threadbare grey cardigan, and she had a warm, kind smile. When she looked at Robert, he felt she could see right inside him.

"Hello, young man," she said. "Can I help you?"

"I was wondering if I could look at the helmet in the window?" Robert asked.

The woman's smile made her eyes crinkle in a friendly way. "Of course," she said. "In fact, you can try it on if you like."

She reached into the window, pulled out the helmet, and dusted it off. Then she handed it to Robert.

"Here you are," she said. "I think it might be just your size."

Robert slipped the helmet over his head. It was dark and felt cool, and the woman was right – it fitted him perfectly. It was as if the helmet had been made especially for him.

Suddenly Robert felt a chilly breeze, and then something heavy on his shoulders. As his eyes adjusted to looking through the visor, he saw the light in the shop change.

"This feels weird," he thought, so he took off the helmet – and looked around,

confused. He wasn't in the shop any more. He was in what looked like the draughty hall of an old castle. And when he looked down, he saw that he was dressed in a suit of armour!

Suddenly a boy in tall boots and a leather jerkin came running towards Robert, carrying a lance.

"Sir Robert!" he cried. "Put on your helmet and take up your lance! The others are waiting for you!"

"Who are you?" asked Robert.

"Don't you recognize me?" asked the boy. "I'm Peter, your squire. You're going on a dragon hunt with Sir Thomas and Sir Daniel, and they're about to leave!"

Robert put the helmet back on, and Peter led him out to the yard, where two knights on horseback – both much bigger and stronger-looking than Robert – were waiting for him.

"Well, at least that hasn't changed," Robert thought to himself. "I'm still a titch compared with everyone else."

Robert mounted his horse, a white pony smaller than the other horses. Even though he had never ridden a horse before, he seemed to know exactly what to do, and he followed the others out of the castle yard and down the road.

"This dragon has been menacing the countryside for weeks," Sir Daniel told him. "The king is counting on us to get rid of it once and for all. And we need your help, Sir Robert."

"How can I possibly help?" Robert wondered out loud.

"Don't be so modest," laughed Sir Thomas. "Everyone knows you are the most skilled dragon fighter in the kingdom!"

Robert was surprised to hear this, but he decided not to say anything else, and the three knights rode on together, with their squires following behind.

They rode through a wood, and then out into a clearing. Beyond the clearing was a bare, craggy mountain with a cave in its side. Thick smoke came from the mouth of the cave.

"That's the dragon's lair," exclaimed Sir Daniel. "We will soon meet our enemy."

The knights did not have long to wait. Just moments later, there was a terrible roar, and flames shot out of the cave.

A moment after that, the dragon itself emerged.

It was horrible – as big as a house and covered with thick green and grey scales. It had broad spiked wings, enormous claws on its heavy feet, and a long neck that could stretch down to the ground. Worst of all, when it hissed at the knights, thick smoke poured from its nostrils, and red-hot flames shot from its mouth.

Robert had never seen anything so terrifying, but it was too late to run away now. He was here, facing the dragon, and his fellow knights were counting on him – though he still wasn't sure how he could help slay this monster.

Sir Daniel rode out ahead, holding his lance in front of him. "Charge!" he called, and the others followed him.

They were all beaten back as the dragon lowered his head and sent scorching flames shooting from his mouth. They were all too big to get beneath the dragon's long, heavy neck…

…all, that is, except Robert. Suddenly Robert knew exactly what he had to do. Leaping from his horse, holding his lance high, he called out to the others, "Keep him busy!"

As the others waved their lances at the dragon, Robert courageously ran right under the dragon's neck, and with all his might, he plunged his lance into the dragon's chest.

The flames stopped. The smoke stopped. With a groan, the huge creature fell to the ground. Robert had slain the dragon!

"Hurrah!" cheered the other knights.

"Hurrah!" cheered the squires.

"Whew!" said Robert. "What a relief!"

The knights rode triumphantly back to the castle. One of the squires had ridden on ahead with the good news, so a welcoming party was already waiting to greet them, led by the king himself.

"Sir Robert," the king said, "you are a hero indeed! The kingdom is in your debt!"

"I am honoured, your Majesty," said Robert. And he got down from his horse and removed his helmet.

Suddenly a cold breeze blew again, and Robert looked around him. His armour had vanished, and he was back in his ordinary clothes, back in the junk shop, with the friendly old woman standing beside him. She smiled down at him.

"That's an amazing helmet," Robert whispered to her.

"It is indeed," she said. "It belonged to a very gallant knight named Sir Robert the Brave. I believe he was smaller than all the other knights, but twice as brave as any of them, and he was a great hero in his time."

"Really? My name is Robert," said Robert shyly.

"Is it?" said the woman. "Well, then I think you should have the helmet. After all, it's just your size."

"Thank you!" said Robert, his eyes shining. "Thank you so much!"

"It's my pleasure," smiled the woman, and she turned and shuffled back into the shadows at the back of the shop.

Robert went outside and picked up his bicycle, putting the helmet in the basket.

As he rode back towards the park, he could see that the five-a-side match was just finishing. He rode over to see how it had gone.

"We got Joe and Ben to make up our side, but we lost by one goal," said Danny. "Ben has to go home, but we can have another match if we can find one more player. I don't suppose you want to play now, do you?"

Robert hesitated for a minute, but then the glint of the helmet in his basket caught his eye.

"Yes," he said bravely. "I'll play."

"Brilliant!" said Danny and Tom. "At last you're playing!"

As Robert joined his friends on the pitch, he felt a little nervous, but every time he glanced over at his bike and saw the helmet gleaming in his basket, he felt much better knowing it was there.

He played well! He kept up with the others, never tripped over the ball, and didn't get trampled in any tackles.

Still, as the end of the second half drew near, his team had only managed a draw. "Just one more goal to win!" shouted Danny, who was in goal for his team.

Robert was at the far end of the pitch when Tom took control of the ball. Tom began charging down the pitch, but he was blocked by two of the bigger boys on the opposing side.

Robert, who had run forward too, knew what to do.

"You're Sir Robert the Brave," he reminded himself. "You can do this!"

Running with all his might, he tore down the pitch, and dodged right between the two bigger boys – he was small enough to get through. Tom swiftly passed him the ball, and Robert blasted it home – right into the back of the net!

Robert had scored the winning goal!

"Hooray!" shouted all his team-mates.

"Hooray!" shouted everyone watching from the sidelines.

"I can't believe I did that!" grinned Robert to himself.

But then he looked over at the helmet, and he did believe it. And he knew that, even if he never grew to be as tall or as strong as his friends, he could still be brave – and a winner.

Iron Jack

Once upon a time, in a land far away, there lived a boy pirate called Iron Jack. He lived with his mum, dad and four older brothers – Dick, Mick, Nick and Rick – on their ship, the *Salty Sue*.

Iron Jack's mum was the captain, and she liked to be called Cap'n Ma. His dad was the first mate. He liked to be called First Mate Pa. And Iron Jack and his brothers were the motley crew. Together they were the roughest, toughest band of pirates that ever sailed the seven seas. Well, Iron Jack's mum, dad and four older brothers were quite tough. Iron Jack was a bit of a softy. He didn't look mean and tough like his family, even though he wore a pirate hat and carried a pirate sword. Beneath his pirate's outfit lay a heart of gold. Iron Jack hated it when they boarded other ships and took people's treasure. He hated fighting and being mean. He was always saying 'excuse me' and 'I beg your pardon' and other soft things that no self-respecting pirate would ever say.

Even Iron Jack's name wasn't quite what it seemed. It wasn't because he was as hard as iron, or carried an iron sword. Oh, no. It was because he was the only one on board the *Salty Sue* who liked to iron! But, even worse than that, Iron Jack HATED sailing. He didn't know his port from his starboard, or his bow from his stern. And, what's more, he didn't care.

While all the other pirates spent their spare time swinging from the rigging or shouting 'shiver me timbers' and 'splice the main brace', Iron Jack daydreamed about life on dry land. He dreamed about living in a fine house, riding a fine horse and wearing fine clothes. He even kept a well-thumbed picture under his pillow of the sort of house he'd like to live in. It was a very grand place, with a long drive and an enormous garden. Every time his brothers saw it, they would laugh. "Why would you want to live there, rather than on the *Salty Sue*?" they'd snort with wonder.

"I can't imagine," Iron Jack would mumble, as the *Salty Sue* rocked from side to side and water dripped on his head from the deck above. And with each passing day, Iron Jack became more and more determined to leave the *Salty Sue*.

Then one day, the *Salty Sue* had just landed in port when Perry the parrot flew aboard with a letter in his beak. Cap'n Ma grabbed it and began to read. As she read, a big smile spread across her face.

"Now listen 'ere, me shipmates," she cried. "This 'ere is from my little sis' – your Aunt Sophie," she added, nodding towards the boys. "She and her girls want to come aboard the *Salty Sue* for a holiday. Now ain't that something. A bunch of landlubbers want to come and stay with us pirates. Now let me see, when are they coming? Oh, here it is. The twenty-fourth of June…now hang on a minute, ain't that today? Shiver me timbers if it ain't!"

Cap'n Ma looked round in panic. They'd just attacked a ship and the *Salty Sue* was in a bit of a pickle. Now, Ma might have been a pirate, but she was a very ship-proud pirate.

"Dick, you swab the decks. Mick, tidy the rigging. Nick, clean out the cannon. Rick, polish the brasses. And Iron Jack, iron the skull and crossbones. While you're all busy doing that, I'll make my famous fish pie and your pa can mix up some pop. We'll give Sophie and her girls a real pirate's welcome."

Iron Jack had just finished hauling up the freshly-pressed skull and crossbones, when he heard the gangplank creak.

"Yoo-hoo," called a ladylike voice. "Anyone home?"

"No one 'ere but us pirates," replied Cap'n Ma, before letting out a very unpirate-like squeal as she rushed to greet her visitors.

Iron Jack's mouth fell open when he caught sight of his cousins. He'd never seen them before and they didn't look at all as he expected. They weren't dressed in pretty dresses. Their hair didn't fall in golden ringlets. And their faces looked grubby. They didn't look at all like land-loving little girls. In fact, they looked just like pirates.

The smallest girl walked up to Iron Jack and stuck out her hand.

"My name's Flo," she said. "The middle one's Mo and the big one's Jo. We're your cousins and we want to be pirates, just like you. Look, we've even got the natty costumes. Mum made them for us specially," Flo added rather proudly.

Jack frowned and looked around for help but his brothers were busy helping Aunt Sophie with her bags.

"Umm…why?" asked Iron Jack. "Why would you want to be pirates when you've got a perfectly nice house to live in and a perfectly nice life on land?"

"Wow! Where should I begin?" asked his cousin.

"Well, first of all there's the *Salty Sue*. Who wouldn't want to live on such a splendid ship? There's the big, wide ocean and the fresh salty sea air. Not to mention all that rigging to swing from. Then there's the fighting and treasure and desert islands. Oh, and did I mention the natty costume?" Flo twirled around in front of Iron Jack, who was looking more and more confused.

Flo was still listing the merits of being a pirate when Cap'n Ma rang the ship's gong for dinner. Ma had prepared a real feast and laid it out on deck. At the centre of the long table was an enormous fish pie. Soon everyone was tucking in.

"Wow, fresh fish pie," cried Flo. "We don't get this at home."

"And we never get to eat outside under the stars, like this," added Mo.

"We're not allowed to eat with our hands at home," added Jo, stuffing a particularly large piece of pie in her mouth.

Later, when everyone had finished eating, First Mate Pa got out his harmonica and began to play a sea shanty. Soon everyone was dancing and singing. Iron Jack and Flo watched as Aunt Sophie, Mo and Jo whirled around the deck, like real pirates.

"You know what?" said Jack, grabbing Flo by the hand. "That does look like fun.

Let's join in." And very soon, Iron Jack was whirling around the deck like a real, fun-loving pirate.

The next morning, the crew of the *Salty Sue* and their visitors rose early. After a hearty breakfast of herrings and toast, Cap'n Ma stood on the poop deck and began issuing orders. "Let's go pirating," she bellowed. "We'll show these landlubbers what being a pirate is all about. Set the sails, splice the main brace and weigh anchor. We've got ships to capture and loot to find."

Soon the *Salty Sue* was speeding across the ocean. And for once, Iron Jack began enjoying himself as he showed Flo, Mo and Jo what ropes to pull and what ropes to coil. He even showed them a treasure map and pointed out all the islands where they had treasure buried. He quite surprised himself with his pirate knowledge. He was just showing Flo how to tie a reef knot when there was a shout from the crow's nest.

"Ship ahoy!" cried Dick. "Everyone to the port side."

"Where?" cried Flo. "Jack, which side is port?"

"Umm…" spluttered Iron Jack, trying really hard to remember.

"To the left," hissed Cap'n Ma, just loud enough for Jack to hear.

"Left," shouted Iron Jack, smiling gratefully at his mum. "Port is left and starboard is right. There, can you see the ship on the horizon?"

Pa fired a warning shot across the other ship's bow. Although Jack and his family were a tough band of pirates, it was the crew of the *Rotten Roger* who were really mean and greedy. They'd often stolen treasure from the *Salty Sue*.

"Right me shipmates," said Ma. "It's time to reclaim our treasure from the *Rotten Roger*." Everyone got excited.

Although *Salty Sue* was a smaller ship, all ships knew that there was no hope of outrunning her. She was the fastest boat on the ocean.

Before long the *Salty Sue* had pulled up alongside the *Rotten Roger*. The crew of the *Salty Sue* stood in line and tossed stinky rotten fish at the other pirates. Iron Jack and Flo took it in turns to see if they could hit the one with the really big nose.

"This really is quite fun," laughed Jack, even though he kept missing.

"Prepare to be boarded, you scurvy swabs," cried Cap'n Ma. And she swung across to the other ship using the *Salty Sue*'s rigging. The rest of the pirates and their visitors were close behind her.

The pirates on the ship, who were now

covered from head-to-foot in stinky fish, took one look at the *Salty Sue* crew and stuck their hands in the air.

"We surrender," shouted the man who looked like the captain.

"Excuse me, may I take our treasure back?" asked Iron Jack.

"Uh, okay," said the captain, who shrugged and pushed a big overflowing treasure chest towards Iron Jack.

"Thank you kindly," said Iron Jack. Then he looked around and blushed. He hoped that Flo, Mo and Jo hadn't heard him being ridiculously polite.

But it seemed that Flo had.

"Wow," said Flo. "You're a real gentleman pirate. That's cool. Perhaps you should be called Gentleman Jack, rather than Iron Jack!"

Jack blushed but didn't say anything as he helped his brothers carry the treasure onto the *Salty Sue*. But later that day, he couldn't help turning the new name over in his head. "Gentleman Jack." It certainly had a ring to it.

That night, Cap'n Ma threw a party on board the *Salty Sue* to celebrate the treasure. Everyone was so happy that they danced and sang until dawn. Iron Jack had never had so much fun. As the sun began to rise over the yardarm, Cap'n Ma called everyone up to the poop deck.

"I've got something to say to you all," she cried. "Today we seized back our treasure that the *Rotten Roger* had stolen from us. There will be piles and piles for everyone. Even you, Iron Jack. You can buy that grand house you are always going on about. Aunt Sophie says that she and the girls will take care of you. Of course we'll all miss you but we want you to live your dream and won't stand in your way." She sniffed loudly and wiped a fat tear from her grubby cheek.

Iron Jack didn't know what to say. He looked at Ma, Pa and his brothers. He looked at the *Salty Sue*. He looked at Flo, Mo and Jo who were desperate to be pirates. He thought about all the fun he'd had with Flo and the others today. Then, he thought back over the years and realized that being a pirate had always been fun. He had just been so busy dreaming about living on land that he hadn't realized it. Slowly, a huge smile spread across his face.

"Thank you, but no thank you," he

declared. "I think I've changed my mind. It's the pirate life for me."

Cap'n Ma rushed up to him and hugged him tightly. "I'm so glad," she cried. "Life on the *Salty Sue* wouldn't be the same without you."

"Hear, hear," cried everyone else. And they all gathered round to hug Iron Jack and pat him on his back.

"Umm…there is just one thing I would like," said Iron Jack, when everyone had settled down.

"What's that?" asked Cap'n Ma. "Do you want more gold?"

"No," laughed Jack. "I'd like you to call me Gentleman Jack, rather than Iron Jack. I think it suits me much better."

"Of course," said Ma. "You're right. Gentleman Jack suits you perfectly." And everyone agreed that she was right!

Clever Dog Snoopy!

Ross opened the window and held the binoculars to his eyes. The view was spectacular. The hotel where he was spending the summer holidays was perched high up on a cliff and he could see for miles. The sun was shining today and through the binoculars everything looked crystal clear. He could see the colours of the deckchairs on the beach below. He could see right into the rock pools where he and his sister fished for crabs, and he could watch the seagulls as they dived off the black rocks which jutted out on either side of the bay.

"Do you want a go?" he said, turning to his sister, Lou.

"OK," said Lou taking the binoculars from him. "Can you watch Snoopy? I don't want him to jump out of the window." Snoopy was their dog. He was small but very lively and seemed to love being on holiday with them.

"Come here Snoops," said Ross, taking the little dog on his lap while Lou leant on the window sill and looked out.

Ross and Lou stayed in the same place every year and loved this wild stretch of coast with its high cliffs, rocky headlands and little bays. The two children loved everything to do with the sea and the beach. They collected shells and made sandcastles. When they weren't swimming or fishing, they pretended to be pirates.

Ross and Lou really loved pretending to be pirates and spent a lot of time exploring the caves at the bottom of the cliffs looking for buried treasure.

"We found a big hole in one of the caves yesterday," Lou had told her mum at breakfast that morning. "There were marks in the sand where someone had dragged a chest full of jewels," added Ross.

Mum and Dad smiled at each other. They were used to this sort of thing. Their two children were always playing pretend games. They just nodded and carried on eating their toast.

Lou and Ross went back to looking through their binoculars. "Ross," murmured Lou, "there's a funny man rowing a boat in the bay."

"What do you mean, funny?" asked Ross.

"He's rowing round and round, like he's looking for something," said Lou.

"Let me see," replied Ross. When he looked through the binoculars, he could see the man clearly, rowing slowly across the

bay, turning the boat
and rowing slowly
back again.

"What if
he is a pirate
looking for
his treasure?"
asked Lou.

"Pirates
don't usually row around in little boats in
the middle of the day," Ross replied. "He's
probably looking for fish or something.
Come on, it'll be lunch soon, let's take
Snoopy for a walk."

The children spent the afternoon on
the beach and forgot all about the man in
the boat. Then, that evening before they
went to bed, Ross was looking through the
binoculars and saw him again. It was
almost dark and the beach was empty. The
man rowed the boat right onto the beach

and jumped out. Then he picked up what looked like a heavy box and disappeared with it into one of the caves.

"Wow!" said Ross.

"What's going on?" asked Lou.

Ross told her what he had just seen.

"So he is a pirate, and he's smuggling treasure."

"Let me see, let me see," said Lou, rather excitedly.

"Hold on a minute…" replied Ross, "he's got back into the boat – and he's rowing away."

He lowered the binoculars and looked meaningfully at his sister, "and he hasn't got the box with him!"

Just then their mum called them.

"It's getting late," she said, "put those binoculars away you two. You'll be able to use them again tomorrow." She kissed them both and turned out the light.

At breakfast the next morning everyone was talking about a burglary that had taken place at a large country house close by.

"Apparently every single item of jewellery was taken," the couple on the next table were saying.

"Some of it was so valuable it was kept in a safe and never worn."

"Family antiques I expect," said someone else.

Ross and Lou said nothing but they were both thinking exactly the same thing. Was the box they had seen being carried into the cave full of the stolen jewels? Was the man in the boat a thief? They couldn't wait to find out.

It was still early when they ran down the private path to the beach but the day was lovely and the sun already felt warm. Snoopy dashed ahead as usual, running in and out of the small waves and chasing the seagulls as they stood at the water's edge looking for worms.

When they reached the caves Lou suddenly hesitated.

"Suppose he's still in there," she said, nervously.

"How can he be," said Ross, "I saw him rowing away last night."

"But he may have come back," Lou replied, looking a bit worried.

While they were talking Snoopy had dashed into the caves ahead of them. Suddenly he started to bark.

"Come on," cried Ross, "Snoopy's found something."

Inside the cave it was cold and dark. The children hadn't brought a torch and it was difficult to see what was going on. Snoopy's barks sounded very loud and when they reached him they saw that he had

started to dig. Sand was flying around him
like clouds of dust and in the hole which
had appeared beneath his scrabbling paws
the children could see something that was
large and black.

Ross knelt
down and felt it.

"Wow! It's
a metal box!"
he cried.

"Let's go,"
said Lou.

Ross was
still prodding
at the box. It was big and heavy.

"I bet this is full of the jewels stolen
from that house that was burgled," he said.
He tried to move it but it wouldn't budge.

"We should go back and tell Mum and
Dad," suggested Lou. "They'll be able to get
it out."

Ross thought for a moment. He really wanted to solve this mystery for himself, but there was no way he could lift the box out of the sand on his own.

"Okay," he agreed, reluctantly.

Mum and Dad looked at each other and smiled when they heard the story of the man in the boat and the box of buried treasure.

"Is this one of your pretend games?" asked Mum.

"No, it's not," Lou insisted with a serious face, "there is a box, and a man, and a boat. Really there is. We think he's a pirate."

"A pirate!" grinned Mum. "Was he wearing a striped T-shirt?"

"And flying the skull and crossbones?" joked Dad.

"It's true," said Lou looking as if she might cry. "There is a box. Snoopy found it.

Come and look, please."

"Alright," agreed Mum, "don't get upset. Wait until this afternoon and we'll all go and look together."

That afternoon as they headed back to the beach, the children ran ahead excitedly. They couldn't wait for the metal box to be opened and the stolen jewellery found. Then everyone would praise them for being so clever.

"There's quite a few caves. Do you know which one it is?" asked Dad.

"Yes, this one," shouted Ross with excitement, and with Snoopy and Lou close behind him, he ran inside. But the children were in for a shock.

The metal box had gone!

Not only that, but the hole where it had been was completely filled in and the sand smoothed over. Ross shook his head in disbelief.

"I can't understand it," he muttered.

Feeling sorry for him, Dad said, "Perhaps you got the wrong cave, Ross. Shall we try the others?"

But it was the same story in the other caves. There was nothing but smooth, wet, undisturbed sand. Lou began to cry.

"We weren't playing pretend," she sobbed, "we really weren't."

"Let's go back and forget the whole thing," said Mum. "We'll take a boat trip. You'll enjoy that."

But not even the promise of a trip to an island could distract Ross's thoughts. He knew he hadn't imagined it. He could still see the black box sticking up out of the sand and feel the cold, sharp edges where he had touched it.

Dejectedly he turned away and followed his parents out of the cave and along the beach. Snoopy, as usual, had dashed ahead, eager to chase any seagulls that might be foolish enough not to see him coming. He ran behind some rocks and Ross could hear him barking.

"Here boy," he called, "here Snoopy." For a moment there was no response, then, Snoopy appeared from behind the rocks and started running towards them, his tail wagging. Ross and Lou could see that something was dangling from his mouth, something bright and shiny, that gleamed yellow in the sun's rays.

Snoopy dropped the yellow object at Ross's feet. Ross bent to pick it up, held it in his hand and looked at it closely. A smile spread slowly over his face.

It was a gold bracelet! "Well done, Snoopy!" cried Lou.

Before they could stop him Snoopy ran off again. This time he appeared trailing something heavy along the sand. It glowed red, like coals in a fire.

It was a beautiful necklace made of sparkling rubies.

For the next half hour the family followed Snoopy around the beach as he dug up small amounts of gold and silver jewellery.

"The thief must have come back for the box and dropped these as he tried to escape," cried Ross, overcome with excitement.

"I think you might be right," replied his dad, "we'll call the police."

When the police arrived, they identified the jewellery and said it came from the burgled house. That night, the police set up an operation to catch the thief. They hid in the caves hoping the man would return to look for the things he had lost. Ross, Lou, Mum and Dad stayed in the hotel and took it in turns to watch what was happening through the binoculars.

Luckily, even though it was the middle of the night there was a bright moon. Lou was the first to see the rowing boat as it came round the headland.

"It's him!" she whispered, "it's him!"

The man dragged the boat on to firm sand and walked up the deserted beach towards the caves, having no idea what was lying in wait for him. The children could see the light of his torch just before he disappeared inside.

For a while there was nothing to see or hear. Ross and Lou could hardly bear the excitement. Then everything seemed to happen at once. Floodlights blazed at the entrance to the cave and figures rushed across the beach as more police piled inside. There was noise and shouting and confusion. They could hear a policeman shouting to the man that he was under arrest. Ross wanted to run down to get a closer look but his parents wouldn't let him.

From the hotel window they watched as the man was led out of the cave with his hands handcuffed behind his back. In the boat the police found the black metal box full of the rest of the jewellery.

The next day a policeman came to visit the children with a reporter from the local newspaper. He wanted to take their photo and write a story about them solving the mystery of the stolen jewellery.

"You see, we really weren't pretending," laughed Lou.

"I'll never doubt you again," smiled Mum, watching proudly as the policeman took it in turns to thank Ross and Lou.

"But Snoopy was the real hero," Ross was telling the reporter. "Nobody believed us at first, so if it hadn't been for him, the missing jewellery might never have been found and the thief would have got away. He really is a clever dog!" and at that everyone agreed.

Snoopy's special reward was a big, red, bouncy ball and for the rest of the holiday he and the children played games with it on the beach. Snoopy loved it so much he no longer cared about chasing seagulls. The children kept an eye out for gold and glinty jewels, just in case...

The Magic Puddles

"Can I help paint the door?" Sam asked his mum. He was really bored because it had been raining all day.

"No, thank you," she said. His mum dipped her brush back in the yellow paint.

"Then can I go to the park?" asked Sam.

She glanced out of the window. "Not yet. It's still raining," she replied.

Sam turned to his dad. "Can I help you paint the wall?"

"Sorry, but no," said his dad. "Oops, watch out! You almost stepped in my paint."

Sam's mum sighed. "Sorry, Sam, but

decorating is quite hard. I'll tell you what. Why don't you paint a picture with some of the left-over paint?"

Sam thought this was a great idea. He grabbed two tins of orange and green paint and sped towards the kitchen.

"Don't make a mess," called his mum.

"Why does everybody always think I'll mess things up?" muttered Sam.

"Because you do," said his sister, Meg, as she passed him. She'd been in the kitchen but decided to leave when Sam arrived, clutching messy paint.

Sam shrugged his shoulders and found a paintbrush. Next he looked for sheets of paper. Sam looked everywhere but there was nothing. He sank down on a kitchen chair, crossed his arms and groaned.

"I can't paint without paper," he muttered. He thought about painting the kitchen cabinets, the wooden chairs, or even the walls. But Sam knew that wouldn't be popular. "I know what I'll paint!" he cried, suddenly having a bright idea.

After half an hour, Sam's wellie boots were covered with orange paint with green stars on top. He put them to dry by the radiator and picked up Meg's boots.

"I'm sure she'll like the same boots as me," he decided, and he got to work with the paint. Meg didn't like it at all.

"What have you done?" she shrieked when she popped into the kitchen.

Meg grabbed a freshly painted boot and ran to find her mum.

"Look what Sam has done!" she shouted.

Mum sighed and looked out of the window.

"It's stopped raining. Why don't you take Sam to the park? That'll keep him out of mischief, and maybe the paint will wash off in the puddles."

Reluctantly, Meg left the house with Sam and off they went to the park. Meg splashed and sploshed through as many puddles as she could find.

"The stupid paint won't wash off," she grumbled.

Sam followed behind. He kept quiet because he knew anything he said would probably make her grumpier.

Meg stomped in another puddle and that's when something really strange happened. There was a great splash and suddenly she disappeared! All that remained were a few ripples.

Sam stared, open-mouthed. He looked frantically around for Meg.

"Meg," he called, over and over again. There was no answer.

Sam frowned at the puddle where he'd last seen Meg. He poked the puddle with the toe of his boot. His orange boot slid deeper and deeper into the water. Sam gulped. Where was the bottom of the puddle? His boot went deeper still and suddenly Sam lost his balance. SPLOSH!

Down, down, down he went – the puddle just kept on going. He felt as though he'd been pushed into the deep end of a swimming pool. He couldn't hold his breath for much longer. His lungs felt ready to burst. Then, suddenly, the water was gone and he could breathe again.

He was standing in another ordinary-looking puddle, but this time the pavement and houses were gone. Instead, he was surrounded by woodland, but he had no idea where he was. Something else was odd apart from his feet feeling soggy in his boots – he was dry. How was that possible? Was this a dream? Sam pinched himself. He didn't wake up.

"Meg, where are you?" he called in a shaky voice.

"Sorry, she ran off before I could speak to her," boomed a voice behind him.

Sam spun round. Standing there was a tiny old man wearing an orange cloak with green stars. The cloak ended just below his knees and he wore orange boots with green stars, just like Sam's.

"I'm Wizard Splosh," he said and shook Sam's hand.

Sam opened his mouth to speak but all that came out was a squeak.

"Ah, you must be in shock," said Wizard Splosh, kindly. "I suppose you didn't realize what would happen if you wore orange boots with green stars and then stepped in a magic puddle."

"A magic puddle?" squeaked Sam.

The wizard smiled. "It's how we wizards travel around. We step in a magic puddle and it brings us out in another magic puddle. It's much more efficient than cars and aeroplanes, and it doesn't pollute the environment."

Sam nodded as though it all made perfect sense. It didn't!

"Now tell me," said Wizard Splosh. "Does that young lady, who arrived first, know what she is doing with magic puddles?"

Sam shook his head. "That was my sister, Meg," he said, trying to sound less like a squeaking mouse. "I'm Sam. I painted the boots, but I didn't realize I'd done anything wrong."

Wizard Splosh patted Sam's arm.

"There'll be no harm done if we catch up with Meg quickly. Now, there's no time to waste. We need to follow your sister so I can send you both home."

"Where did she go?" asked Sam, gazing around. All he could see were trees and puddles. The puddles looked muddy, not magic.

"Well, only a few puddles are magic," explained Wizard Splosh. "Meg must have stepped in another magic puddle. Don't worry, I just need to do a small spell and we'll be able to find it."

Sam felt himself

nod in agreement. Everything was so weird he decided he might as well go along with it. What else could he do? And he had a bad feeling that this mess was his fault.

Wizard Splosh took Sam's hand and chanted what Sam thought must be a spell.

"Splish, splash, splish, splash.
Find a puddle – in we dash."

All of a sudden, amongst all the muddy puddles, one puddle shone orange with sparkling green stars.

"That's the nearest magic puddle," declared the wizard. "I hope it's the one your sister stepped in."

He sprinted off and jumped in the shimmering puddle, pulling Sam behind him.

SPLOSH!

This time Sam knew what to expect, so

he didn't panic at the strange feeling of falling through water.

Out they came, onto a wide grey tarmac, covered with hundreds of puddles. Once again, Sam didn't feel wet, apart from some water in his boots, but overhead, a deafening noise bellowed and shrieked. Sam covered his ears. He looked up and got quite a shock.

A huge aeroplane was coming in to land, and they were standing on the airport runway! The wizard yelled:

"Splish, splash, splish, splash.
Find a puddle – in we dash."

In the distance a puddle glittered orange and green. They ran. Sam had never run so fast. He thought his head would split open with the noise of the plane pounding through his skull.

Together they leapt into the puddle and suddenly the deafening noise stopped.

Instantly all was calm and hushed and very, very dark. In fact, this time they couldn't see anything. Absolutely nothing. Sam waved his hand in front of his face. There wasn't a flicker of movement.

"We must be deep down in a cave," said a voice from the blackness.

"But caves don't have puddles," replied Sam worriedly.

"Listen," whispered Wizard Splosh. "Can you hear the water dripping? This cave must flood when it rains outside. There will be puddles all around us; we just can't see them."

"Meg! Are you there?" called Sam.

"Meg! Are you there?" an echo bounced back.

He called again, a little louder. The echo called back, a little louder. But there was no real voice. He was beginning to get pretty scared.

In the blackness Sam felt the wizard take his hand. Then he heard the familiar chant:

"Splish, splash, splish, splash.
Find a puddle – in we dash."

There, just in front of them, a shining orange and green puddle dazzled their eyes.

They jumped.

SPLOSH!

Out they came into blinding sunshine. In front of them was clear blue sky, rocks, bright flowers and lots and lots of sand.

"Now where are we?" asked Sam.

Before Wizard Splosh could reply, Sam yelled, "Meg!"

A girl was standing on a huge rock in front of them, looking very lost. It was Meg.

"Sam!" she cried in a croaky voice.

Meg ran to her brother. They hugged and Sam could hear quiet sobs from his sister.

"This must have been very frightening for you," said a voice.

Meg's head jerked up and she noticed the wizard for the first time.

"What…?" she started to say.

"Sit down," said Wizard Splosh, kindly. "Let me explain what magic puddles are."

"I'm really sorry, this mess is my fault. I painted our boots orange with green stars and that activated the magic puddles," Sam said.

"I don't care, Sam." Meg said after she'd listened to Wizard Splosh.

The wizard patted Sam's arm.

"Anyway, it's not every day an ordinary child gets to discover the magical world. Now, we just need to find one more magic puddle," he said, looking around. "Then, if you step in it, holding your boots, you'll be transported back to the first puddle of the day."

"There might be a problem," said Sam in a small voice.

"Nonsense," said the wizard, and he chanted:

"Splish, splash, splish, splash.
Find a puddle – in we dash."

They gazed around.

"We're in a desert," said Sam. "Deserts don't often have rain and puddles."

"Are we stuck here forever?" wailed Meg in dispair.

"No," the wizard assured them. "It does rain occasionally, and we travelled here in a puddle…" he looked around, and his face suddenly fell.

The three of them looked around to see the magic puddle they came in, but the puddle had evaporated in the hot sun.

"Oh dear," said Wizard Splosh. "I'm sure we'll be able to find a magic puddle somewhere," the wizard muttered.

Sam clambered up a rock. The wizard said the magic spell again and Sam stared out across the desert. He squinted as far as he could see. For a moment he thought he saw an orange shimmer, but it was only a bush with orange flowers.

"We'll have to explore further," said the wizard, mopping his brow in the heat.

When Sam jumped down from the rock, the water in his boots sloshed around. He stood still.

"I've got an idea," he grinned.

"Please can it be a good one," mumbled Meg, who was starting to feel really thirsty.

"My boots are full of water from the magic puddles. Maybe all our boots have water in them. Could we empty out the water to make a new magic puddle?"

"Yes!" cried the wizard, clapping his hands together. "That's an excellent idea."

"First, we need to find a good place to make the puddle," explained Sam.

They searched the ground for a good place. Finally, Sam pointed to a rock with a big dip in it, just large enough for three people to stand in.

Carefully, the three of them emptied puddle water from their boots into the rocky basin.

"It doesn't look like enough water," said Meg.

Wizard Splosh wrung out his sock to get a few drops more.

"That should be enough. Now step in, before the sun dries up the water."

Sam, Meg and the wizard stood in the puddle, holding their boots and soggy socks. Sam secretly wished that his plan would work. He even missed the rain at home. He closed his eyes shut and waited for wizard Splosh's chant.

"Splish, splash, splish, splash.
Return us home in a flash!"

When Sam opened his eyes again he found himself with Meg standing in an ordinary-looking puddle, outside their local park. There was no Wizard Splosh and the only strange thing was the fact that they were in bare feet, holding their boots and socks.

"What just happened?" a puzzled Meg asked.

"We travelled through magic puddles. There was a wizard…" Sam replied.

Meg nodded, then she shook her head as though to get rid of a weird dream.

"Let's go home."

That afternoon Meg used paintbrush cleaner on her boots to clean off the orange paint and green stars. She noticed Sam didn't. Sam shrugged his shoulders and grinned. "It'll keep me from getting bored."

"But be careful," Meg said. And she never mentioned magic puddles again.

Annie and the Egyptians

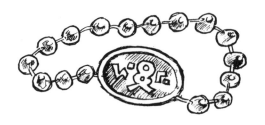

W hat a funny shop, thought Annie, pressing her nose to the window. She could barely see anything through the cobweb-covered glass. I'll just pop in. Mustn't be long…got to be home for tea, she thought to herself, as she turned the creaky door handle. A bell tinkled as she entered a dimly lit room and an old man appeared from the shadows.

"May I help you?" asked the old man, peering at Annie through thin-rimmed spectacles. "Anything catch your eye?"

"Oh!" said Annie, glancing around the teetering piles of chipped china and dusty ornaments. She was hoping to find something that might help her with her school project, which was all about Egypt. The teacher had told the class to write a story about the Egyptians and Annie didn't know where to begin.

Suddenly, Annie's gaze fell on a string of brown beads in the shop. It looked a bit Egyptian. "I like that old necklace."

"That," replied the man, "is not just any old necklace. It is an heirloom. Belonged to my father, that did. Brought it back from his travels. He was a very famous explorer."

"Then why are you selling it?" asked Annie, puzzled.

The old man's eyes narrowed. "Ah," he said. "It's caused a spot of trouble, you might say...but that's all in the past," he added, hastily.

Annie ran the necklace through her fingers. The beads were worn and knobbly. In the middle of the string was a larger oval bead scratched with what might be some kind of writing. "This is perfect. I'll take it!" she exclaimed, giving the old man some of her money.

Soon Annie was skipping down the road with the old beaded necklace around her neck, thinking of what she could write about in her story. The street was crowded with shoppers and Annie weaved her way in and out, past a busker with a penny whistle and on towards home. She checked her watch. Should be in time for tea, she thought.

Just then she came across a wonderful sight: a woman sprayed from head to toe in gold and dressed as an Ancient Egyptian. Annie was fascinated by the sight of this woman. She stood still in front of a cardboard cut-out pyramid that was propped against a tree behind her. It almost looked as though she was guarding an entrance to a real pyramid.

As people passed, if anyone dropped a coin into the plate at her golden feet, she raised her arms and did a dance, then after they'd gone she stopped and  stood motionless again.

Annie was entranced. She felt in her pocket for the change from her necklace and bent down to put a coin in the plate. But as she did so, instead of raising her arms to dance, the Ancient Egyptian lunged forwards and grabbed at her necklace.

"Thief! You've stolen the pharaoh's

sacred amulet," she cried. Annie tried to step away from the woman but she had gripped the beads so tightly and was dragging Annie towards the pyramid's cardboard entrance.

"The pharaoh will hear of this!" the golden woman shouted. Annie didn't know what to do. She tried to step away from the woman and shouted for help but she and the woman seemed invisible to all the passers-by.

The woman's golden fingers were trying to loosen Annie's hold on the beads. Then she pushed Annie through the pyramid's cardboard doorway and the next thing she knew she was in a hot, dark, narrow corridor.

"Help!" cried Annie, but her voice trailed off into black emptiness. I must run, she thought. With all her strength she freed herself from the golden woman's grasp and sped off down the corridor, covering the necklace protectively with one hand. She passed a flaming torch on a bracket above her head and noticed by its light that the walls were covered in hieroglyphs!

On and on she ran, until at last she realized that she was heading straight for a man, dressed just the same as the woman.

"Oh, no!" Annie said to herself, but to her astonishment, the man pressed himself flat against the wall to let her pass, then sprang forward to block the way to her pursuer.

"Stop!" she heard him growl. "No one except royalty beyond this point."

"Why didn't he stop me?" Annie wondered. She still had a hand across her necklace and looked down to check that it was unharmed. To Annie's amazement, she found that she was no longer wearing her T-shirt and jeans, but a white sleeveless gown, embroidered with gold thread, that reached the floor. On her arm was a heavy, jewelled bracelet. She was dressed as an Egyptian princess!

Annie had stopped running and had arrived at the entrance to a magnificent room. Lanterns illuminated the walls, which were painted with pictures. Annie immediately recognized them as scenes of Ancient Egyptian life from her school project.

The air was heavy with perfumed clouds of incense, but at the far end of the room, seated on a golden throne, she could see the pharaoh! Luckily, he was listening to one of his courtiers and didn't notice Annie, who had dived for cover behind a gilded couch.

She was still catching her breath, when she heard "Pssst!" in her ear. Right beside her was a boy of about her own age

– an Egyptian boy. He had a pleated white cloth wrapped around his waist and a wide metal collar around his neck. And he was staring at Annie's beads with a look of wonder and surprise. Before Annie could speak, he pressed a finger to his lips.

"Shhh! Don't move or we're in trouble, Princess!" he hissed.

"Princess? Who are you?" whispered Annie.

"I'm Tut, the pharaoh's servant. Right now, I don't want him to see me – or you! Now, follow me or they'll catch you." Then, seeing Annie's anxious look, he added, "I promise I won't hurt you."

Tut wriggled on his belly away from the couch and towards an opening in the wall, through which Annie could see palm trees and in the distance, the silvery waters of a river. That must be the river Nile, she thought to herself.

Annie followed Tut and soon found herself standing outside in the hot Egyptian sunshine.

"We can hide here," said Tut, darting behind a great lotus-topped pillar covered in ancient hieroglyphs. "As soon as I saw you, Princess, I realized you were wearing the amulet."

"Amulet?" said Annie. "I don't understand!"

Tut was pointing at her neck. "Your necklace. It belongs to the pharaoh!" he cried. "He always wore it and then he lost it one day. There's a huge reward for whoever finds it because it's so special."

"That must have been why the woman was chasing me," thought Annie. "But why are my beads special?" she asked.

"The scratches on the amulet are thought to be a riddle," said Tut. "As soon as the riddle has been solved, the amulet magically guides its wearer to a secret door which leads to the world beyond the sky. The pharaoh had the best brains in all of Egypt working on that riddle until he lost the amulet. That's why he's so desperate to get it back. And why anyone who sees you wearing it will try to take it from you."

"Whatever shall I do?" wailed Annie. "I just want to go home!"

"If you give me the amulet," said Tut, "I'll help you find the world beyond the sky."

Annie wasn't sure whether to trust Tut. But what choice did she have? Besides, there was a chance that the world beyond the sky might actually be her only means of getting home. Maybe it was the escape route out of Ancient Egypt. It was worth a try.

She slipped the beads off her neck and handed them to Tut. He let the beads slip through his fingers, just as Annie had done in the shop. Suddenly, Annie realized! The father of the old man from the shop must have been the explorer who brought the beads back from Egypt. The pharaoh must have been trying to get them back ever since!

"There's no time to lose," said Tut. "The pharaoh has people searching everywhere for the amulet. Others who have worn the amulet have solved the riddle before and I think I can too."

"I found this in the pharaoh's throne room," Tut continued, fishing out a scrap of

paper from a hidden
pocket in the folds
of his tunic. "I
think it's a code."
Annie thought it
looked peculiar.
Someone had used
a ballpoint pen to

write on the lined paper. Annie knew that
the Ancient Egyptians used papyrus and
ink, not paper and biros!

She took a closer look at the crumpled
paper. There was a line of hieroglyphs and
a translation underneath that read:

To seek the world
Beyond the sky.
Look in the Nile
Where it is dry.

Someone had obviously translated the hieroglyphs in neat handwriting.

But then it began to make sense. The explorer must have found the amulet and worked out the code of scratches to translate the riddle. If only Annie could solve the riddle too!

"It's ridiculous," she said. "How can the River Nile be dry?"

"Come on, follow me! I've got an idea," said Tut, walking towards the water. Soon they found themselves in front of the Nile.

"Look!" whispered Tut, peering in the river. "We can see our reflections in the water and we're dry, aren't we? I reckon this might be a clue to solving the riddle!"

So, Annie and Tut tiptoed along the bank, taking care not to fall in. They kept stopping to look at the reflections around them in the water. At last, they saw something twinkling in the ripples.

Annie looked up and saw that a golden key was dangling off one of the branches on a palm tree directly above them. Tut hopped about with excitement.

"We've done it!" he whispered.

"Have we?" whispered Annie.

"Yes, I can feel the amulet pulling me! The secret door must be this way." Once again Tut grabbed Annie's hand and led her across the sand towards the pyramids.

The amulet guided them into the shade of one side of a pyramid. Now Tut was scrabbling at the stones in front of him, tugging at them with his bare fingers.

"Oh, which one? Which one?" he muttered.

At last, one of the stones came loose. Annie could see that in the gap left by the stone was a door. The secret door. Tut's fingers trembled as he tried the golden key in the lock.

"It fits!" he cried, as he carefully turned it. Click! Tut put his shoulder to the stones and pushed. The secret door in the wall opened inwards and the pair of them tumbled through.

"You go on alone, Princess. You must hurry quickly and make your way to the top," said Tut.

"But aren't you coming too?" asked Annie.

"No," said Tut. "My place is here. I must go back and return the amulet. Goodbye and good luck in the world beyond the sky!" Then he turned and was gone.

Annie shivered. It was dark and creepy inside the pyramid. Now that Tut had gone she felt lonely and scared. The adventure was starting to sink in and she was worried people at home would think she was missing.

She started to run. She ran up and up,

getting higher and higher. "I must get back home!" she thought, running faster and faster.

Annie could see light in the distance. She ran towards it, knowing it must be the sky through the top of the pyramid. As she reached the opening she closed her eyes tightly and flung herself as hard as she could through the hole.

When she opened her eyes again, she found that she was standing on the pavement in the shopping centre by the cardboard pyramid. Her Egyptian clothes were gone and she was dressed in her old T-shirt and jeans. She felt around her neck for the string of old brown beads, but remembered Tut had them, and would return them to where they belonged.

Annie looked at her watch. Not a moment had passed since when she had been standing there last. It was as if she had been there all along.

Annie thought about Tut, the pharaoh, and the amulet, and then Annie smiled.

"I know exactly what to write in my story now," she thought. And she hurried home in time for tea.

Jamie's Secret

"Oy, over here, Jake!" Jamie yelled, running as fast as he could up the football pitch.

It was a very cold afternoon and Jamie was playing in a match for his club, Forest United. His twin brother, Jake, was also playing.

Jake dribbled the football past the opposition towards the goal area. He looked up and spotted Jamie just in front of him, but decided to take the shot himself. Jake kicked the ball high up in the air so that it soared past the bewildered goalkeeper and into the back of the net.

"Goal!" Jamie's teammates cried,

racing forward to congratulate Jake.

Jamie scowled in his brother's direction and kicked the ground in frustration. Why hadn't Jake passed the ball to him? He was in the perfect position to score. It was so typical of Jake to keep all of the glory for himself.

"It's just not fair," Jamie mumbled. "I'm supposed to be the team striker too. Why won't Jake pass the ball to me?"

Jake was the star player of the football team and whenever he had possession of the ball, he never seemed to want to get rid of it. Or that's what Jamie thought anyway.

Jamie was so deep in thought that he didn't notice a player from the opposition run straight past him with the ball, and it wasn't long before the other team scored a goal, levelling the match.

"Get with it, Jamie, or we'll lose the game," Jake shouted from the other side of the football pitch.

Later on, with three minutes left to the final whistle, the score was still one all.

Suddenly, Jake took control of the ball and began to dribble it back up the pitch towards the goal.

"Jake!" Jamie cried out again, getting himself into another good position near the goal. But it seemed as if his brother hadn't heard him at all. Jake ran ahead of Jamie and aimed the ball in the top left-hand corner of the net.

"He shoots, he scores!" Jake yelled, as the ball flew past the poor goalkeeper for a second time. Moments later, the referee blew the final whistle.

Jamie's side had won the game, thanks to his twin brother.

Almost everyone in the team hugged and congratulated Jake, including his mum and dad. They didn't seem to notice Jamie standing alone.

"We're so proud of you," Jamie overheard his mum tell Jake.

"Aww, Mum, get off! You're embarrassing me," Jake replied. But Jamie could see that he looked really pleased.

"If only Jake had passed the ball to me," Jamie thought, angrily. "Then maybe I could have scored the winning goal and Mum and Dad would be proud of me too."

Jamie didn't think that anyone would

notice if he just disappeared out of sight. So, without another thought, Jamie ran towards the old clubhouse near the entrance to the playing fields.

When he got there, Jamie barged inside and headed for the changing room.

"Don't you want something to eat first, dear?" an old lady called after him.

She was busy putting out sandwiches for the two teams to eat when they returned from the pitch.

"No thanks, I'm not hungry," Jamie replied, opening the changing room door.

Jamie untied the laces on his football boots, then sat down and tried to shake them off his feet without using his hands. Suddenly, his left boot flew up high in the air and landed on something in the far corner, which was covered by a dustsheet.

"Ouch!" said a muffled voice beneath the sheet. "What do you think you're playing at?"

"Oh, no! I must have hit someone with my boot," Jamie thought, his heart sinking.

"S-s-sorry, I didn't realize anyone else was in here," he called out, walking towards the mound of lumpy white material. When Jamie pulled back the sheet, a very old football table stood beneath it.

Jamie hadn't noticed it in the changing room before. Someone must have put it there recently.

He looked closely at the table. There were rows of tatty old plastic football figures, joined together by silver rods with rubber handles at each end. The players were wearing a mixture of blue and red football shirts.

"Now I'm just imagining things," Jamie muttered under his breath. "There's no one in here but me and this stupid table."

He turned one of the handles half way around, which flipped a row of red-shirted players upside down. Then, Jamie picked up his own football boot from the floor and walked back towards the bench.

"Hey," said another voice. "You can't just leave us up here like this! We've got a match to play!"

Jamie slowly turned around and faced the table again. This time he knew he hadn't imagined voices.

He walked up to it and looked at the row of plastic legs sticking up in the air.

"Well?" said one of the football figures nearest to where Jamie was standing. "Are you going to turn us around or not? I'm beginning to feel a bit queasy."

Still shocked by what he was seeing, Jamie twiddled the handle back round the other way so that the figures were standing upright again.

"Ah! That's better. Do you want to play a game of football with us?" the same red-shirted player asked Jamie, taking him by surprise.

Jamie thought he must have been dreaming, or maybe he had bumped his head in the match when he headed the ball. He pinched himself hard just to make sure. "Ouch!" No, he definitely wasn't dreaming and the football players were all still looking at him.

"Uh, sure, I'll play, but I've got no one to play against," Jamie replied, looking at the empty space in front of him on the other side of the table.

"Hey, you've got a whole team to play opposite," chuckled another player.

Jamie was confused. He didn't understand what the football figures were talking about. He rubbed his eyes and blinked, hoping it would all make sense when he opened his eyes again.

But when Jamie did open them, he found that he was no longer looking down at the football table from above, but rather he was on it.

"Huh?" he gasped, looking at the players all around him. They didn't seem to be attached to metal rods any more and Jamie was now the same size as them! Even the pretend pitch looked real.

"Right, what position do you want to play?" asked a player in a blue shirt.

"Er, striker," said Jamie, thinking of the position he played normally.

"Well," the blue-shirted player replied,

"we don't have specific positions for this game. You're either an attacker, a defender or a goalie. So, what will it be?"

Jamie chose to be an attacker. He was given a blue shirt and told to stay up front.

There didn't seem to be a star player in either the blue or the red teams, and everyone liked passing the ball to each other. Jamie even scored a couple of goals!

Suddenly, Jamie heard the door to the changing room swing open. He blinked and found himself in front of the table, back to his normal size again.

"Jamie, what are you doing in here?" It was Jake, followed by the rest of the team.

"Yeah, why didn't you come and eat the sandwiches?" asked another teammate. "The coach made a speech and your brother won 'Player of the Match'."

"What, again?" Jamie muttered under his breath.

Realizing that the football table was still uncovered, Jamie hastily tried to pull up the dustsheet before anyone could see it. He wanted to keep this as his secret.

But Jake had seen it. He walked over to where Jamie was standing.

"What are you hiding under there?" Jake whispered to his brother? Jake lifted up the dustsheet and grinned at Jamie.

"Wow! Table football," he continued. "It looks pretty old and rusty. I wonder if it still works."

Much to Jamie's annoyance, Jake rattled the handles roughly as he turned the plastic football figures around.

"Careful!" said Jamie. "You might hurt them..."

"Hurt who?" Jake asked, confused.

"Oh, n-no one," Jamie stammered. "I, er, I meant the table. I didn't want you to break the table."

"Come on," Jake sighed, "Mum and Dad are probably looking for us. Let's get dressed and go home."

From that day on, Jamie tried to visit the clubhouse as much as possible to play table football. Every time he took the sheet off the table, Jamie magically found himself in the middle of the pretend pitch, as if he were one of the players.

One day, just before a real match at the club, Jamie arrived at the changing room earlier than normal so that he could play a game of table football before kick-off.

But Jamie couldn't see the dustsheet or the football table anywhere. They seemed to have vanished just as quickly as they had appeared.

Disappointed, Jamie slowly got dressed in his team strip and waited for the rest of the players to arrive.

"You left early this morning," said Jake, as he sauntered into the changing room a while later. "What's the rush?"

"Nothing," Jamie replied, grumpily.

Jake looked at his brother and sighed.

"I hope you're going to be in a better mood when we play football. This game's very important. We wouldn't want to lose today," he warned.

Jamie glared at his brother.

"What difference would it make if I

didn't play?" he snapped angrily. "You never pass the ball to me anyway. You might as well play the game all by yourself."

And with that, Jamie stormed out of the clubhouse, stomping across the playing fields towards the pitch where the opposition was just beginning to warm up.

As soon as the game started, Jake didn't seem to hog the ball as much as usual. In fact, he didn't appear to be doing anything much at all. The other side scored within the first five minutes.

"Jake, what are you doing?" called the coach from the sidelines. "Get out there and score a goal."

Even Jamie was beginning to worry about Jake.

"What's wrong?" Jamie asked his brother at half time. "Don't you want to be the hero of the game today?"

"No, I don't," Jake said, sadly. "I didn't

realize that was how you felt until earlier. So, I thought I'd hang back a bit and give you a chance to score the goals."

Jamie looked at his brother and shook his head in exasperation.

"But don't you see?" he replied. "Just by doing that, you're still not being a team player. It would be much better if we played together."

Jake shuffled his feet on the ground for a couple of seconds.

"Well, okay then," he finally agreed.

In the second half of the match, Jake almost immediately got the ball and dribbled it towards the goal.

"Over here," Jamie called out to his brother. And this time, Jake looked up, saw Jamie, and passed the ball to him. With one eye on the ball and the other on the goal, Jamie kicked the ball as hard as he could. It flew over the goalkeeper's head, narrowly missing the goalpost, and went into the back of the net.

"GOAL!"

Jamie's teammates all rushed forward to give him a hug. But first in line was his twin brother, Jake.

"You did it mate!" he beamed.

"No, we did it," Jamie corrected him.

For the rest of the game, Jamie and Jake worked together as a team, scoring another two goals between them.

Jamie's club Forest United finally won the match three goals to one.

This time, when the final whistle blew, Jamie's mum and dad ran onto the pitch to congratulate both of their sons.

"I didn't realize you were as good a footballer as your brother, Jamie," grinned his dad, full of pride.

"Well," Jake smiled, putting his arm around his twin brother, "that's probably because he never got a chance to show off his skills before."

After the match, Jamie snuck off to the clubhouse to find the table football players. He wanted to tell them all about the game and him scoring.

When he got to the changing rooms he found a pile of chairs stacked up where the table football had been. Just then, his brother Jake came in.

"What are you looking sad for Jamie? You just won the match," Jake said, giving his brother a friendly shove.

"Oh, nothing," Jamie replied, still wondering where the table football had gone. "I just fancied a game on the table football. Have you seen it?" he asked.

"Oh yeah, I asked the coach about that," Jake replied. "It belongs to the old lady who makes the sandwiches in the clubhouse. Apparently, it's been in her family for a while and she wanted somewhere to store it while she was moving house."

"Oh," Jamie sighed, disappointed. He wished that he'd had a chance to say goodbye to the players.

"According to the coach, the old lady said I could go around to her house to play a game or two. Apparently, the plastic football figures miss me!" Jake chuckled, wiggling his finger around in a circle to suggest the lady was slightly crazy.

Jamie smiled. The old lady must have

mistaken Jake for him. They did look alike, being twins and all.

"Yeah," Jamie grinned, feeling happier again. "Imagine that! Talking football figures, eh? Who would have thought it?"

And off they both went, with Jamie already planning his visit to the old lady's house.

Moon Rescue

Tom Mason pulled on his space boots, snapped his helmet shut, then dropped through the airlock onto the Moon's dusty surface.

Ahead, he could see the Space Academy's silver building, a short distance from Moon Station 3 where he lived. He would have to hurry – he was going to be late for his Saturday job.

Tom had recently moved to the Moon with his family, and he loved it. He loved wearing his white padded spacesuit with its shiny helmet and big moon boots. He loved the feeling of being weightless when he was outside the Moon Station and was able to leap really high, right over the big space rocks that littered the Moon's surface. He loved gazing back at the Earth, which glowed green and blue in the blackness of space like a round, bright jewel.

Most of all, he loved watching the spacecraft zip in and out of the Space Academy. Tom was mad about spacecraft. He had got the Saturday job cleaning at the Academy, so he could see the spacecraft up close. There were giant cargo-carrying supercruisers, medium-sized cruisers that could carry people to and from Earth, and small shuttles that ferried staff around the various Moon Stations.

Recently everybody had been talking about the Space Academy's latest spacecraft, a tiny, two-person jetpod. Tom hadn't yet seen it in real-life, but he had a poster of it on his bedroom wall. It looked amazing and was supposed to be the fastest thing the Space Academy had ever built.

Tom's dream – which he wanted more than anything else in the entire Solar System – was to become a space cadet and train at the Space Academy, so he could learn to fly spacecraft like the jetpod. But by the time Tom had moved to the Moon, the Space Academy had been full, so there were no more places left for any more cadets.

One day, Tom was tidying up one of the training rooms at the Space Academy. It was full of flight simulators – a different kind for each spacecraft. The space cadets learnt to fly on these, in preparation for flying the real craft when they were old enough.

The room was usually empty by the time Tom arrived and he had never seen any of the simulators in adventure. Today, however, a technician in a white lab coat was lying underneath a new flight simulator, alongside a box of tools.

"Ah, pass me a wrench, would you?" he called.

"Me?" asked Tom, spinning round in surprise.

"Well there's no one else here," said the technician grumpily. "Pass the one with the red handle, and press the green button on the side of the simulator, while you're at it."

Tom did as he was told, then watched, fascinated, as the flight simulator's lights flickered on and the machine began to whirr.

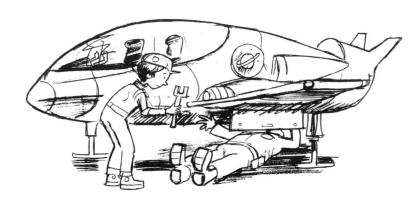

ADVENTURE STORIES

"Thank you," said the technician, straightening up. "It's not good for my old bones lying on the floor like that."

He peered at Tom from under a pair of white bushy eyebrows.

"I've not seen you around here before. Are you a cadet?"

"N...No..." stammered Tom. "My name's Tom...Tom Mason. I'm at school on Moon Station 3. I just work here on Saturdays...you know...to be near the spacecraft."

"Ah, so you like spacecraft do you?" said the technician, smiling. He held out his hand to Tom. "I'm Bill Woodward," he said. "Pleased to meet you!"

"I know your name, sir," said Tom, shaking Bill's hand. "You designed the jetpod!"

"That's right," replied Bill, "Like it, do you?"

"Oh, yes," said Tom, eyes shining. "It's magic!"

"Well, we're going to be training the space cadets to fly it soon, once I've got this jetpod simulator up and running," he explained. He patted the flight simulator's side, then looked thoughtfully at Tom.

"The space cadets are all away on a training mission. Do you fancy helping me get this simulator up and running, so it's ready when they get back?" he smiled.

"You bet, sir," replied Tom with a grin.

"Right," said Bill. "Put on this helmet and strap yourself in. The chair moves around so it feels as though you're really in a spacecraft."

Bill quickly ran Tom through the controls. "The control stick is really sensitive," Bill warned, "so you need a light touch. Ready?"

Tom nodded. Bill flipped a switch and

a curved screen in front of Tom's chair lit up showing a view of the Academy's take-off and landing bay, with the Moon's surface beyond.

"It's realistic, isn't it," chuckled Bill. "Okay, let's go!"

Tom switched on the engines and gently raised the control stick. Immediately, he felt his chair hover as if he really was in a tiny spacecraft. Then he pushed the stick forward and he was off. The whole simulator swung wildly to the left and right as Tom got to grips with the controls, but he soon got the hang of it.

On the screen in front of him, he could see the ground rushing past as he made the craft go faster and faster. Obstacles began to appear and he had to fly over big boulders, navigate long rock tunnels, and avoid flying space rocks. An hour passed in no time at all.

"That's amazing..." Bill was muttering to himself as Tom took off his helmet. "Could you help me out again, tomorrow, Tom? I want to fine-tune the controls and the computer software."

"Yes please, sir!" said Tom. "That would be great!"

The next day, and for the next few evenings after school, Tom helped Bill test the jetpod flight simulator. Bill programmed it so Tom had to try out different levels of difficulty and fly through all kinds of obstacles, sometimes with one engine down, or with one of the controls not working properly. Tom sailed through it all.

"You're a natural, Tom," said Bill, one

evening, after Tom had just completed level 20.

Just then an alarm sounded.

"What's that?" gasped Tom.

"I've no idea," frowned Bill. "Come on. We had better go to the Control Room!"

In the Control Room, Space Academy flying officers and engineers were gathered in front of a huge screen watching a flickering image of the Academy's Space Commander.

"Engines not responding...I repeat, engines not responding..." the Commander was saying over the crackle and hiss of static. "Doors jammed fast. I cannot get out. I repeat, I cannot get out..."

"What's going on?" Bill asked one of the flying officers.

"The Commander dropped the space cadets off on the far side of the Moon for a training mission," replied the officer. "But his cruiser had engine trouble when he was flying back to the Academy. He's crash-landed!"

"Where?" Bill gasped.

"Cassini Crater – and it doesn't look good," the officer spoke in a low worried tone. He pointed to his computer screen, which showed a satellite image of the Commander's craft, dangerously balanced on the rim of the crater.

"That crater's more than 10,000 metres deep. If the cruiser goes over the side, it'll be smashed to pieces!"

"There's something else," interrupted one of the engineers. "There's a meteor shower on its way. It will reach the Cassini Crater in…" he paused, frantically keying numbers into his computer, "…20 minutes."

There was a stunned silence.

"If one of those space rocks hits the

Commander's cruiser..." began the engineer.

"...yes, we know," interrupted the officer, grimly. "It will tip the cruiser right into the crater. We've not much time. We've got to send out a rescue spacecraft."

"But all our craft are too heavy," the engineer shook his head. "If they try to dock with the Commander's spacecraft, they'll both go over the side..."

"The jetpod could do it..." Tom piped up. "It's fast and light – and it's the only spacecraft fast enough to dodge meteors."

"But no-one has been trained to fly a jetpod!" exclaimed the engineer.

"Someone has," Bill explained. He turned to Tom.

"Will you help?" he asked.

"Of course. But how...?" Tom began.

"Follow me!" Bill cried, grabbing Tom's arm. Together they raced down the corridors of the Space Academy to the docking bay, past rows of supercruisers, cruisers and shuttles. Right at the end, in a small bay by itself, was a gleaming, brand-new jetpod.

"Right, are you ready?" asked Bill.

"M-m-me…?" stammered Tom.

"Yes, you. You're the only one who can do it! You've flown missions like this on the simulator lots of times."

Tom didn't stop to think. He grabbed a helmet, climbed in the jetpod, and strapped

himself in.

"I'll be in the Control Room," yelled Bill. "Good luck, Tom!"

The jetpod's door swished shut.

Tom couldn't believe it. He was actually in a real jetpod! He took a deep breath, switched on the engines and raised the control stick. The jetpod began to hover. Tom pushed forward the familiar control and, within seconds, was blasting out of the Space Academy.

"Tom, can you hear me?" called Bill, through the speaker in Tom's helmet.

"Loud and clear, sir!"

"I'm going to tell you how to set your course for Cassini Crater."

"Yes, sir!"

"Estimated time of arrival — 16 minutes."

Tom punched in the course setting radioed by Bill. The jetpod felt just like the simulator, so he tried not to think about the fact he was really speeding through space. Eventually he saw the crater below him, a huge shadowy hole in the Moon's surface. The Commander's cruiser was teetering on the edge, like a tiny insect about to tumble in.

"Right, Tom," said Bill. "You've got 60 seconds until that meteor shower hits. Go for it!"

Tom used thrusters to slow down the jetpod until it was hovering over the Commander's cruiser.

"40 seconds!" called Bill.

Carefully, Tom lowered the jetpod until the hatch door on its base was lined up with hatch door on top of the cruiser.

"20 seconds!"

Tom leaped out of his chair and slammed the handle to release the lock on the hatchdoor in the jetpod's floor.

"10 seconds! 9...8..."

The hatch door shot upwards and the Commander hauled himself on board, banging the door shut behind him.

"...7....6...5..."

Tom dived back into his seat and pressed a button to detach the jetpod from the cruiser.

"...4...3...2..."

The jetpod shot upwards as the weight of the cruiser dropped away below. Out of the window, Tom and the Commander saw it slide over the rim of the crater and hurtle down the crater's steep side.

"1...GET OUT OF THERE!" yelled Bill, as hailstone-sized lumps of rock and ice began clattering on the roof of the jetpod.

"Strap yourself in, Commander!" yelled Tom, "It's going to be a bumpy ride!"

Tom set his course for the Academy but now they were in the thick of the meteor shower, and the space rocks were getting bigger.

A huge meteor caught the side of the jetpod, making it spin wildly, but Tom managed to grab the control stick and get back on course.

"Engine No. 1 is down," shouted the Commander, as lights began to flash on the control panel.

"Don't worry," yelled Tom, through gritted teeth, "I've done this before…"

Tom began to weave in and out of the falling rocks, flying the spacecraft as fast as it would go. He and the Commander were flung from side to side as he steered the spacecraft left, then right, then up, then down, using all his skill and powers of concentration. Far below, they could see clouds of dust explode into the air as meteors smashed into the ground.

Then, all of a sudden, the jetpod shot out of the meteor shower into the stillness of space, and they could see the stars again, shining white against the inky blackness.

"Five minutes until touchdown, Commander," said Tom, setting his course towards the Space Academy.

The Commander was staring at him.

"You're not one of my space cadets!

Who are you?"

"Tom Mason, sir!" replied Tom.

"Well, good flying, Tom Mason," grinned the Commander, shaking his head in wonder. "Take us in!"

Back at the Academy, a huge cheer went up as Tom and the Commander climbed out of the jetpod.

"Well done, Tom!" yelled Bill, slapping Tom on the back.

"Tell me, Tom," said the Commander. "Where did you learn to fly like that?"

"On the jetpod flight simulator, sir," replied Tom. "I've been helping Mr Woodward test it."

"It's true, Commander," explained Bill. "The boy's a natural."

"Yes, he certainly is," agreed the Commander.

They all looked at the jetpod. It's shiny, new surface was scratched and dented all over.

"It's looks terrible," said Tom, sadly.

"...but it still flies like a dream!" replied the Commander. "Don't worry. We're getting a delivery of 50 brand new jetpods next week. What do you think, Bill? Do you think we could spare one as a thank you gift for our brave young pilot?"

"I should think so, Commander," agreed Bill, smiling.

"R-r-really?" stammered Tom, his mouth open in astonishment.

"Really," confirmed the Commander, "but on one condition. You start training as a space cadet first thing next week. I need pilots like you in my squad. Are you in?"

For a moment, Tom was speechless, then he leaped up, punching his fist in the air for joy.

"Yes, sir!"

The Laughing Ghost

Not many people lived in a home like Patrick Brown's. When Patrick took the bus home after school, he got off where the road ran closest to the river and walked the short distance along the riverbank to an old iron bridge. Crossing this, he reached an island in the middle of the river. And that's where Patrick lived, in a houseboat.

The boat was called *The Good Aunt Hetty*. It was long and narrow, and had seven cabins joined by a passageway. The roof over the cabins was strong, and had a rail all round, so it was quite safe to play on – and you could see everything that was going on.

Once, long ago, the boat had travelled up and down the river, pulled along from the towpath by two horses. Now it had two engines. Sometimes Patrick's mum and dad threw off the mooring lines that held the boat to their jetty, and they would putter away on *The Good Aunt Hetty* to see other parts of the world – even if they were very small parts of the world, and not far away.

Patrick loved everything about the river. His two best friends, Dan and Sally, lived on boats moored not far away, and there were always lots of interesting things to look at.

It was a busy part of the waterway. Patrick and his friends could roam the island, visit each other's boats, kick a ball around, or just watch the world go by. As long as you could swim and were sensible, it was the best place in the world to grow up. Even the old hotel was not off-limits.

The hotel had been empty for a long time. It stood in the centre of the island and had once been very grand. There was even a theatre inside, where long ago, famous people had appeared. Now the hotel was empty.

The island children had once played inside, putting on shows for their parents and the other boat owners. But the once dazzling-white hotel was now a grubby grey colour, and it had quite a spooky feel about it, so no one went inside any more.

Patrick's dad was reading the paper when Patrick came home from school one Friday afternoon. Patrick was pleased to see him because he had some important news, but before he could speak, his dad began:

"Patrick, listen to this! It says in the paper that a man wanted by the police has been seen hanging around this area. He's stealing rare wild animals, and he raids the nests of rare birds, too. He sounds like a nasty piece of work."

Patrick gasped. "It could be that new man on the island. The one with the bent nose, and he's got a scratch on his face. I bet one of the animals he was trying to pinch scratched him!" he exclaimed.

"Do you mean Carl Smith?" replied his dad. "He seems all right to me. Whatever makes you think he could be this criminal?"

"I passed his boat yesterday," Patrick explained. "When he saw me, he threw something big in the water. When I looked, it was a swan. It was flapping around in circles like it was tied up, and its feathers looked messy."

"I'm sure there's a reason for what you saw," frowned Patrick's dad, "but still..."

As soon as he could, Patrick found Dan and Sally. First they talked about the animal-smuggling story, but then Patrick remembered his really important news. It had gone completely out of his head.

"Oh, I forgot to say! I found a ghost!" Patrick told them.

"A ghost? I don't believe in them," replied Dan, scornfully.

"Well, I didn't find one exactly..." Patrick hesitated. "I heard one when I was walking home. It had a scary laugh that came from the old theatre."

"Wow! Perhaps it's the ghost of a famous old actor!" Sally suggested.

"Hmm. More likely it was just a telly on too loud," Dan added, doubtfully.

"I'm sure it wasn't, and I'll prove it," Patrick declared…

That evening, Patrick, Dan and Sally sat in the main cabin of *The Good Aunt Hetty*, trying to persuade his mum to let them sleep outside, on top of the deck.

"I'm not sure I like the idea of you lot sleeping out in the open," his mum said.

"We want to hear the night sounds, Mum," Patrick pleaded.

"And look at the stars," added Sally.

"Oh, okay. I'll make you all a nice hot drink," Mum insisted. "You must use plenty of insect spray, and take blankets to put on top of your sleeping bags. You'd be much more comfortable inside, you know…"

"It'll be great, Mrs Brown," put in Dan.

"It's an adventure!"

"Well, yes, I suppose it is," Mum agreed, "but wrap up warm – and you must come down off the roof if the weather turns bad, and…"

"Thanks, Mum!" Patrick cried, and jumped up to get things ready before she could change her mind.

Darkness came late at this time of year, and it was still light when they got to bed up in the open air. They slipped into their sleeping bags but it wasn't cold. The sky was scarlet where the sun was setting. It was a very beautiful place to live and it was hard to believe anything bad or scary could happen there.

"Has everybody got backpacks and torches?" Patrick asked, as if he had a large squad of explorers under his command. The other two nodded.

"Mum has lent me her alarm clock,"

Patrick explained. "I couldn't tell her we were listening for a laughing ghost. She thinks we need it for owl-watching and stuff. I've set it to wake us at three o'clock."

"Okay then," said Dan. "Give me a kick at three."

It was dark by the time they all got to sleep, but it seemed no time at all before the alarm went off. It sounded so loud, Patrick was afraid the whole island would think it was time to get up, but although a dog started barking, no one else seemed to have noticed.

It was pitch dark now, and had become much cooler. The three friends sat up, glad of the extra blankets, which they pulled around themselves. They sat quietly for a little while, just listening. Two owls called to each other nearby, and then a nightingale started singing in the tall tree growing by the towpath next to them. Its song was lovely, but very loud too.

"We'll never hear a ghost with this going on," groaned Sally. "We have to get closer to the hotel."

They'd prepared for this. They pulled on outdoor clothes over their pyjamas, and crossed the roof, tiptoeing so Patrick's parents wouldn't hear them below. Then they lowered themselves from the roof by the cabin wall-ladder and hopped onto the jetty. It only took a minute to cross the rough grass and the old hotel car park that lay between the boat and the theatre end of the hotel.

As soon as they got close they heard the laughter. It did sound scary, like a loud man's laugh, and it definitely didn't sound like a TV left on.

"See?" whispered Patrick looking at his friends. "I was right, wasn't I?"

"I'm scared!" cried Dan, suddenly believing very strongly in ghosts! "Let's get nearer the windows," whispered Sally. "Look! there's a light! Oh, It's gone off now. There's someone in there!"

Nervously, they moved nearer, holding their torches high. They didn't notice the four large metal dustbins until they kicked them over. They made a terrible racket; the lids fell off and clattered in circles, and one rolled right across the car park, down the bank and into the water. The sound went on for ages. Then all the dogs on the island started barking!

The children turned and ran, and didn't stop until they'd clambered back on board *The Good Aunt Hetty*.

"What's going on up there?" Dad called from inside the boat.

"Nothing," wheezed Patrick, short of breath. "We thought we heard a noise so we got up. Er, I think we might come inside now, if that's okay."

Next morning the three friends had an early breakfast and then went out so they could talk.

"I couldn't go inside the hotel last night," Dan shook his head. "No way. Not in the dark."

"Nor could I," admitted Sally, "and the window was too high to see through anyway."

"Let's investigate now — in morning

daylight!" Patrick exclaimed.

The three friends continued round to the other side of the hotel where the main entrance stood. The hotel was not so crumbling that it was unsafe, and the door was unlocked, so they let themselves into the foyer and closed the door behind them. But the lights didn't work and the shutters

were all closed, so it was pretty gloomy, even though it was morning. They went through the door behind the hotel desk and found themselves in a maze of corridors that turned this way and that, until they hadn't a clue where they were.

Then they all heard the scratching sounds.

"This is really, really scary!" Dan whispered.

"I'm a bit spooked too," admitted Sally.

In the end, it was the scratching sounds that led them to the room they were looking for. The sign 'THEATRE' was carved upon the door. Slowly, they eased it open and peered in. The shutters in the theatre were wide open – sunlight almost blinded them.

There were rustlings and cheeping from the big room, and the three adventurers could see rows and rows of cages. The first one they came to was large and Patrick immediately recognized the occupant.

"It's the swan I told you about! I knew there was something bad about that man…" he declared. "What's he done to it? Look at the poor thing. It's all twisted up!"

They looked at more cages. They all had animals in them, and they all looked in poor condition. There was a scruffy owl, a long animal that they couldn't recognize, a coypu, a little mink that hissed at them, ducks, water voles, a badger, an otter, and lots more.

They walked down the aisles, until they finally got to a cloth-covered cage. Sally pulled the cloth away, and a sleepy green parrot blinked at the light…and began to laugh.

It was such a jolly sound, and now that they knew it wasn't human, it no longer sounded so spooky. They joined in the laughter, relieved they hadn't met a ghost…so they didn't notice the large man behind them, filling the doorway.

"Well now. I thought I might find you here," said a deep voice.

Sally, Dan, and Patrick jumped at the sound. Frightened speechless, they turned towards the intruder.

"I'd like a word with you," said Carl Smith.

There was a horrified silence. Patrick found his courage first.

"These animals…they're all hurt, or sick," he said, trying to sound brave. "They shouldn't be here!"

The man just smiled.

"Oh, I agree with you," he said. "I do try my best but I have more patients than I can cope with."

"Patients?" asked Sally, weakly.

"This is my animal hospital. I've begun patrolling the river and I bring in sick or damaged creatures, and treat them here until they recover. Then I put them back," Carl Smith explained.

"But I saw you throw a swan into the river. It didn't look as if it had recovered!" Patrick blurted out.

"No, she was struggling too much for

me to hold and she got away. She'd got tangled in a fishing line and her wing was broken. I caught her again later. She's doing all right now, but the wing will take time to mend."

"What about the parrot?" gabbled Sally nervously. "Parrots come from jungles, not rivers!"

"Well, some parrots do live wild here now. This parrot comes from Westley Park, just upriver. There's a colony of green parrots there and sometimes they get attacked by other birds. I get them regularly here, to nurse better. They make me laugh and they copy the sound, so apparently the park is full of laughing parrots, all sounding like me!

"Look, it's quite difficult looking after so many animals and birds. That's why I wanted to talk to you, to ask for your help. I can tell you all care about animals.

Maybe you could come by every now and then and help out? I know the animals would like it. Would you consider it?"

Later that day, Carl Smith sat with Patrick's mum, dad, and the three adventurers on board *The Good Aunt Hetty*. He told them that he'd helped the police to capture the animal thief just the day before.

"I think he might have been trying to catch our swan," Carl explained. "He won't be bothering the river animals again, thank goodness."

"I'm sorry. I thought the animal thief might be you," Patrick admitted, feeling ashamed. Carl didn't mind.

"That tells me you're vigilant as well as brave," he said. "You're definitely the right kids to help me in my hospital."

The three friends were really excited that Carl had asked them to help look after the animals, and they couldn't wait to see them again.

Especially the laughing green parrot, who they nicknamed 'Ghostie'!

The Amazing Atlas

Twins Tabitha and Jack were just finishing their cornflakes at the breakfast table when their mum told them the news.

"Dad and I have arranged for you to have a little holiday while we move house," she said, clearing away the empty bowls. "Aunt Agatha has offered to have you for a few days. She lives in the village next to the one where our new house is."

"Who's Aunt Agatha?" asked Jack. "I've never heard of her."

"Yes, you have," replied his mum. "She looked after you when you were babies. She's not really your aunt, though. She's one of your grandma's friends."

"Well, I can't even remember what she looks like," said Tabitha.

"I don't want to go and stay with some stuffy old aunt," growled Jack crossly. "There won't be anything to do there…"

"Aunt Agatha is definitely NOT stuffy," laughed their mother. "She's a very interesting old lady. She's travelled all over the world."

"I bet her house smells of moth balls," muttered Jack, under his breath.

"Don't be rude," said his dad. "It's not open for discussion. "It's all been arranged. I'm going to drop you both off tomorrow morning."

It was raining hard as the car pulled up in Aunt Agatha's driveway the next morning. Tabitha and Jack gazed out of the window glumly. The rambling old house looked dark and spooky in the rain, and the garden was a tangle of overgrown bushes.

"There's Aunt Agatha," smiled dad, waving through the car window. The twins turned to look, expecting to see a grey-haired old lady, dressed in a cardigan and woolly skirt. But they were in for a surprise.

There on the doorstep stood a tall thin woman with wild red hair, wearing a purple velvet dress. She wore a brightly patterned scarf draped round her shoulders, and a long necklace of big blue beads. From a distance, it was hard to tell exactly how old she was. It was only when they got closer, Tabitha and Jack could see how wrinkled her face was.

"I hope she doesn't try and kiss us," whispered Jack, as they got out of the car.

"Behave, Jack," warned his dad.

"Come inside," called Aunt Agatha, holding open the door as they all dashed in, out of the rain. "I'm sorry I couldn't arrange for better weather for your visit."

Feeling slightly awkward, Tabitha and Jack smiled politely as Aunt Agatha showed them where to hang up their coats.

"It's been such a long time since I last saw you," smiled the strangely dressed old lady. "I won't try and kiss you, though. I hate being kissed by people I don't know, don't you?"

The twins grinned. Despite themselves, they couldn't help liking Aunt Agatha.

"Well, I hope you don't mind entertaining yourselves," said Aunt Agatha, sweeping the two children into the house again, after waving goodbye to their dad. "I'm afraid I'm not much good at playing these days. And I don't expect you really want me to play with you, do you?"

The two children laughed. "Where are we allowed to go?" asked Tabitha, trying to be polite.

Aunt Agatha looked surprised. "Why, anywhere you like!" she exclaimed. "I don't have any silly rules in this house. All I ask is that you leave me in peace and quiet for my morning rest. Why don't you start by exploring the house?"

"Brilliant!" cried Jack. "We love to explore."

"It sounds like you are both born explorers, just like me," beamed Aunt Agatha. "Can I suggest you start in the library? You'll find all sorts of exciting things in there. It's just down the corridor on the left." And with that, Aunt Agatha retired into the sitting room, and closed the door.

Jack and Tabitha wandered off down

the corridor.

"I don't see what's so exciting about a library," said Jack, as Tabitha pushed open the big oak doors. "They're just full of musty old books."

Sure enough, the walls were lined with endless shelves, loaded with dusty volumes with strange titles.

"*Seven Years in Tibet*," read Tabitha, pulling one of the books off a shelf.

"Fascinating, I don't think," laughed Jack. "This one sounds more like it – *The Forbidden City*. I wonder why it is forbidden?"

"Hey, Jack! Come and look at this," called Tabitha, who was turning the pages of what looked like a battered old atlas.

"What's so interesting about a boring old atlas?" asked Jack, leaning over her shoulder. "It's falling apart."

"Look!" replied his sister, ignoring his

comment. She pointed at some words written in red ink, across the top of the page. "I wonder who wrote this?"

"'Where do you want to go?'" read Jack, tracing the sentence with his finger. "How about, here!" he cried, stabbing the page with his finger.

Suddenly, there was a tremendous FLASH of light. It was so bright that Tabitha and Jack had to close their eyes tightly. When they opened them again, they could hardly believe what they saw.

Instead of Aunt Agatha's dark, dusty library, they found themselves sitting up a tree in the middle of what looked like a swamp. All around, they were surrounded by lush green overgrowth. Below them swirled a muddy river. The air was filled with all sorts of strange, unfamiliar noises.

"What was that?" gasped Tabitha, as a loud shriek rang out.

"More to the point, how did we get up here?" asked Jack.

"It must be the atlas," replied Tabitha, she was still holding it in her hands. "Somehow, this old book has transported us to the place you pointed to on the map. Where did you choose?"

"I don't know," shrugged Jack. "I think it was somewhere in Africa."

"That's just great!" cried Tabitha. "We're up a tree, in a swamp, somewhere in Africa!"

"Don't blame me," said Jack crossly. "How was I to know Aunt Agatha keeps magic books in her library?"

It wasn't long before they both realized that arguing wasn't going to get them very far.

"We need to try and work out where we are," said Tabitha sensibly. "Let's open the atlas again, and look at the map."

"I think I pointed about there," said Jack indicating a rough area on a map of Africa."

"That's West Africa," said Tabitha knowledgeably. "That makes sense. There are lots of swamps there. They're called the Mangroves. Mr Brookes was telling us in our geography lesson. Maybe if you'd been paying attention in class you'd know!" she added sarcastically.

"Well done, Einstein," said Jack. "Did they also teach you how to get down from a

Mangrove Tree?"

Tabitha frowned. "Well, we can slide down these," she said, pointing to the tangle of what looked like vines, dangling down from the branches. "They're actually tree roots," she added. "They take in oxygen from the air."

"Thanks for the lesson," said Jack. He was starting to secretly wish he did pay more attention in lessons. Tabitha always knew everything, which was annoying when you're a twin.

They slid down the roots and landed with a bump at the base of the tree. "Let's go, all those weird noises are giving me the spooks," he added, starting to miss Aunt Agatha's boring house.

Tabitha nodded. "Come on, then. The water doesn't look as deep here. Maybe we can wade down river until we reach firmer ground." And with that she started to wade into the muddy swamp.

"STOP!" cried Jack, grabbing hold of his sister's arm. He pointed to a shoal of small brown fish, lurking in the shadows.

"So what?" said Tabitha. "They're only little fish!"

"PIRANHAS, you mean," corrected Jack. "I'm sure they would love a bite of your leg, given half a chance."

Tabitha leapt out of the water in a flash. "Thanks," she gulped. "Now what are we going to do?" Jack couldn't help feeling a bit pleased that he knew something his sister didn't.

Just then, Jack spotted something in the bushes on the other bank.

"Look over there!" he cried. "It's a boat. We can't be that far from civilization. If we could just reach it, we could float down the river to safety."

Tabitha agreed. "We could sit on one

of these logs, and paddle across to the boat."

Between them, the twins hauled a huge log into the water. Tabitha tucked the ancient atlas under her arm, and the two children climbed on board.

"Sit still!" complained Jack, as the log rolled one way, then the other in the water.

"I can't help it!" yelled Tabitha. "It's not easy doing this, and holding an atlas you know. Stop moaning and paddle as quickly as you can! NOW!"

"What's the hurry?" asked Jack, looking round. Then he saw what Tabitha had seen. A long dark shape was slowly making its way towards them through the water. Jack could just make out a long snout and two nostrils breaking the surface.

"C…c…crocodile!" cried Jack, pulling his feet out of the water in a panic. The log lurched dangerously from side to side. Tabitha just managed to save herself, but the atlas shot from under her arm and landed with a SPLASH! in the water. The crocodile was getting closer and closer.

"Help me!" shouted Tabitha, leaning out as far as she could to reach the atlas. Jack held on tight to his sister's other arm as she struggled to grab the book before the fast approaching crocodile arrived. Sensing movement in the water, the crocodile opened it's enormous jaws, ready to bite. SNAP! Just as Tabitha grabbed the book, the crocodile's jaws closed on the corner, ripping out a huge bite.

"Paddle like crazy!" yelled Tabitha, thrusting the atlas into Jack's hands. Jack plunged the atlas into the water and used it to paddle.

"Where's the crocodile now?" he shouted, turning round to Tabitha.

His sister shook her head, "I don't know," she replied breathlessly. "It must have gone underwater."

"Perhaps it doesn't like the taste of dusty old books!" suggested Jack. Whatever the reason, the crocodile did seem to have gone. As quickly as they could the twins made their way across to the other side of the swamp. Taking care not to fall in, they climbed into the boat, and set it adrift.

"I'm soaking," announced Tabitha.

"So is the atlas," said Jack, laying it down in the boat. "And it's got a huge bite out of it. I don't think Aunt Agatha will be very pleased when she sees it again."

"IF she sees it again," said Tabitha. "How do we know where this river goes? We might end up anywhere."

"Don't worry, Tabs," joked Jack. "At least we've got an atlas to show us the way."

Suddenly, Jack's face broke into a huge grin. "That's it! Why didn't we think of it before," he cried. "The atlas! It brought us here, so it can take us home again. Quick! Find a map of England."

Tabitha carefully turned the wet pages, until she found what she was looking for. Sure enough, across the top of the sodden page, written in very blurry red ink were the words: "Where do you want to go?"

"Little Muckle," cried Tabitha, pointing to a tiny dot on the map. "That's Aunt Agatha's village. We want to go there now!"

FLASH! In an instant the two children found themselves standing outside Little Muckle Post Office in the pouring rain.

"We'd better get home before we are missed" said Tabitha, her voice full of relief. "They've probably sent out search parties for us by now."

"I don't know how we are going to explain this one," said Jack as they trudged up the drive to the house. "No one will EVER believe us! Maybe we can sneak in without being seen."

But as they came round the corner, there was Aunt Agatha, standing on the doorstep.

"I know we've been gone for a long time, but we can explain…" began Tabitha, holding out the sodden atlas guiltily. But to her surprise, Aunt Agatha didn't appear to hear her. In fact, she looked totally unconcerned.

"Oh, hello again," she said, her eyes twinkling. "I was just looking for Mouser, my cat. Did you have fun in the library?" Her eyes stopped to rest on the dripping book in Tabitha's hands. "Ah," she beamed. "I see you found my atlas. I do so love looking at my atlas. SO educational, I always think. Why don't you try the History section tomorrow?"